101+ *Secrets*, **FACTS**, and *BUZZ* about the **STARS** of

HIGH SCHOOL MUSICAL

CORBIN

ASHLEY

ZAC

VANESSA

By Michael Anne Johns

SCHOLASTIC INC.

New York   Toronto   London   Auckland   Sydney
Mexico City   New Delhi   Hong Kong   Buenos Aires

Photo Credits

ISBN-13: 978-0-545-03475-3
ISBN-10: 0-545-03475-2

Copyright © 2007 Scholastic Inc.

All rights reserved. Published by Scholastic Inc.
SCHOLASTIC and associated logos are trademarks and/or registered trademarks of Scholastic Inc.

12 11 10 9 8 7 6   7 8 9 10/0

Designed by Two Red Shoes Design
Printed in the U.S.A.
First printing, June 2007

TABLE OF CONTENTS

Introduction 4

Zac Attack!: Zac Efron 5

All about Vanessa: Vanessa Anne Hudgens ... 11

All about Ashley: Ashley Tisdale 17

Crush on Corbin!: Corbin Bleu 22

The Luck of Lucas: Lucas Grabeel 27

Monique Mania: Monique Coleman 32

Cookie Cutey: Chris Warren, Jr. 37

Spotlight on Andrew Seeley 40

Introduction

No one ever **imagined** the *High School Musical* **phenomenon** when the Disney Channel TV movie debuted January 20, 2006! Sure, it combined a **fun, fun, fun** script with Kenny Ortega, who is one of Hollywood's most respected choreographers and directors, with a cast of **TALENTED HOTTIES AND HONEYS**, with a soundtrack that was guaranteed to keep you singing along . . . but . . . the response was definitely **over the top!**

The **largest EVER audience** for a cable TV original movie, with the numbers exploding with every repeat airing! The soundtrack CD zooming to the **tip-top** of the *Billboard* charts! Singles from the CD **busting** onto *Billboard*'s top 10 lists the very first day of release! The **stars** — Zac Efron, Vanessa Anne Hudgens, Ashley Tisdale, Corbin Bleu, Lucas Grabeel, and Monique Coleman — appearing on the **covers of magazines** from *Tiger Beat* to *Teen People*! Articles in **MAJOR** publications such as *Newsweek* (10 pages!!!), *Rolling Stone*, and *The Wall Street Journal*!

Well, with **MILLIONS of fans** all over the world, *HSM* has turned into part of teens' and tweens' lifestyles. From T-shirts, to DVDs, to CDs, to school drama productions, *HSM* is **here to STAY!** And, of course, if you're a **TRUE-BLUE**, dyed-in-the-wool, *High School Musical* fan, you probably know **stacks of fax** about the movie, the cast and crew . . . but on the following pages you will find **BUNCHES-OF-BITS** you never knew about the stars *and* some tidbits about *High School Musical 2*. Read on, and you just might be the **trivia-star** at your next *High School Musical* **theme** party!

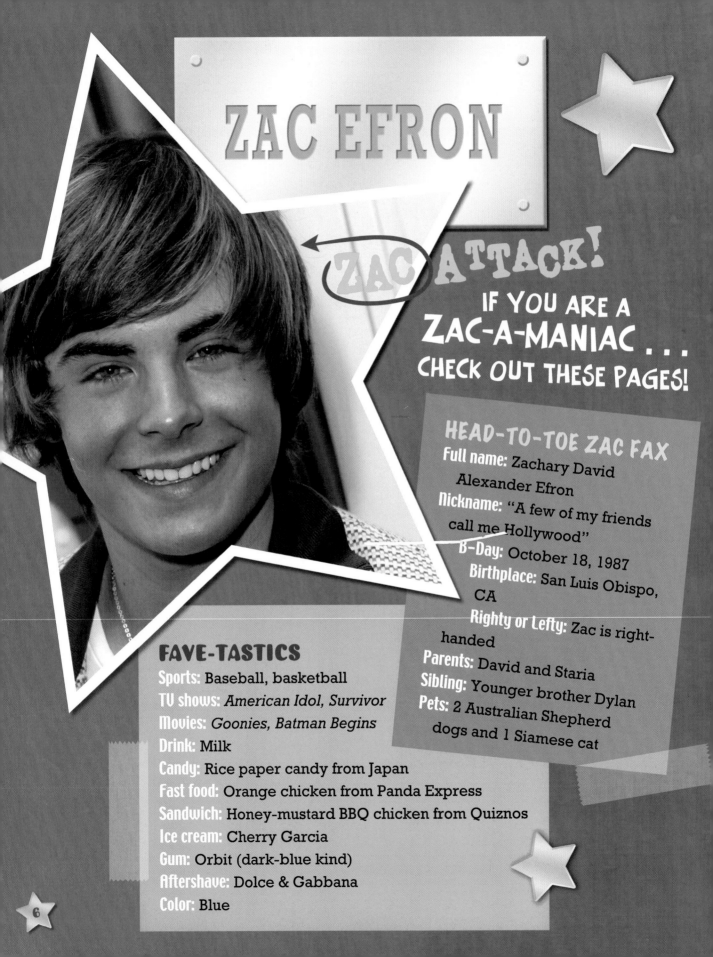

ZAC EFRON

ZAC ATTACK!

IF YOU ARE A **ZAC-A-MANIAC** . . . CHECK OUT THESE PAGES!

HEAD-TO-TOE ZAC FAX

Full name: Zachary David Alexander Efron

Nickname: "A few of my friends call me Hollywood"

B-Day: October 18, 1987

Birthplace: San Luis Obispo, CA

Righty or Lefty: Zac is right-handed

Parents: David and Staria

Sibling: Younger brother Dylan

Pets: 2 Australian Shepherd dogs and 1 Siamese cat

FAVE-TASTICS

Sports: Baseball, basketball

TV shows: *American Idol, Survivor*

Movies: *Goonies, Batman Begins*

Drink: Milk

Candy: Rice paper candy from Japan

Fast food: Orange chicken from Panda Express

Sandwich: Honey-mustard BBQ chicken from Quiznos

Ice cream: Cherry Garcia

Gum: Orbit (dark-blue kind)

Aftershave: Dolce & Gabbana

Color: Blue

Zac — Australian-Style:

When the *HSM* cast went Down Under to promote the movie, Zac described it as a "dream come true! ... We met nice people, ate all the food, played didgeridoos [local musical instruments] and went to the zoo!"

COSTAR QUICKIES ⭐
Zac's instant response to his castmates:

Vanessa: "Hot"
Ashley: "Sweet"
Corbin: "Big hair" [laughs]
Monique: "Energetic"
Lucas: "Chill"
Troy Is the Boy: "Troy Bolton — cool guy, super-jock extraordinaire and, boy, I wish I were more like my character," says Zac. "Troy meets Gabriella on vacation and there's a connection. And when they come back to school, they have to sort of break through each other's peer groups in order to come together."

ZAC'S POV ON THE SEQUEL:

"I would like to do more dancing in the new one — there were a lot of numbers that my character missed out on in the first one. I loved when people were doing flips and cartwheels on cafeteria tables; it looked like so much fun."

ZAC'S TEEN SURVIVAL GUIDE

ON THE FIRST DAY OF SCHOOL... "Your **first impression** on your teacher is a big one, so make it good — because they're gonna help you out later in the year. I've learned that from **experience**, I haven't bribed a teacher, but I make sure to give them **gifts** on all the holidays. I'm the one who every morning says, 'Good morning, Miss So-and-So, how are you?'"

IN HIGH SCHOOL ENGLISH CLASS... Zac **impressed** his teacher Laura Wade — "He was able to follow through on all his assignments and never expected **preferential** treatment."

IN SCHOOL... "I was **never** the cool kid. I was always sort of a bookworm. I always try to get the best grades, and I'm **proud** of that."

BEING WITH MY FAMILY... "is a **treat.** You have to remember as you grow up that friends will always stick by you, but **your family** even more so. Your family will always be **inside your** heart and by your side — no matter what."

ZAC-CLOPEDIA

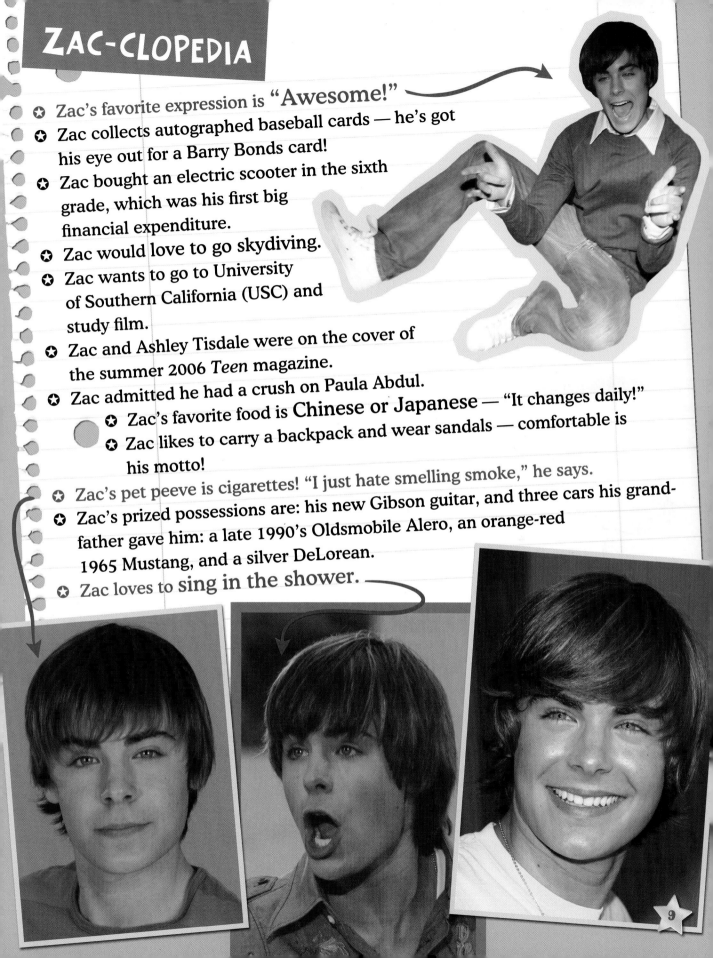

- Zac's favorite expression is "Awesome!"
- Zac collects autographed baseball cards — he's got his eye out for a Barry Bonds card!
- Zac bought an electric scooter in the sixth grade, which was his first big financial expenditure.
- Zac would love to go skydiving.
- Zac wants to go to University of Southern California (USC) and study film.
- Zac and Ashley Tisdale were on the cover of the summer 2006 *Teen* magazine.
- Zac admitted he had a crush on Paula Abdul.
    - Zac's favorite food is Chinese or Japanese — "It changes daily!"
    - Zac likes to carry a backpack and wear sandals — comfortable is his motto!
- Zac's pet peeve is cigarettes! "I just hate smelling smoke," he says.
- Zac's prized possessions are: his new Gibson guitar, and three cars his grandfather gave him: a late 1990's Oldsmobile Alero, an orange-red 1965 Mustang, and a silver DeLorean.
- Zac loves to sing in the shower.

ZAC . . . NEXT!
Zac is playing the role of "Link Larkin" in the movie *Hairspray*. He will be costarring with John Travolta, Nicole Blonsky, Amanda Bynes, Queen Latifah, and Michelle Pfeiffer.

ZAC'S HOMETOWN:
Arroyo Grande, California. Midway between Los Angeles and San Francisco. Arroyo Grande means "big ditch" or "big stream." Arroyo Grande was founded in 1832.

ZAC, ZAC, SUPERSTAR!
Success is fun for Zac, but not all-consuming. "I'm so excited to have it," he says. "I just can't get caught up in it."

TCKET
ADMIT ONE

VANESSA ANNE HUDGENS

ALL ABOUT VANESSA

CALLING ALL VANESSA FANS ... READ ON!

VANESSA'S VITAL STATS

Full name: Vanessa Anne Hudgens
B-Day: December 14, 1988
Birthplace: Salinas, CA
Heritage: Filipino, Chinese, Latina (from her mother) and Irish and Native American (from her dad)
Parents: Greg and Gina
Sibling: Younger sister Stella
Pets: 1 toy poodle named Shadow; 3 turtles; fish; 1 bunny

FAVE-TASTICS

Musicals: *Phantom of the Opera*, *Gypsy*
Pastime: Shopping
Stores: Planet Funk, Urban Outfitters
Childhood book: *Goodnight Moon*
Tween book: *A Child Called It*
Movie: Tim Burton's *The Nightmare Before Christmas*
Kinds of movies: Scary movies
Type of guy: "I like cute, funny, sweet guys, loyal and honest. I like guys with long hair, but not too long."
Actress: The late Natalie Wood
Prized possession: Her family
Car: Porsche Carerra GT
Cartoon series: *SpongeBob SquarePants*

VANESSA'S POV:
For her *HSM* Audition: Vanessa sang Jessica Simpson's "Angels"

On Gabriella:
"She is kind of the brainy girl who just likes to cuddle up with a good book. And I like playing the role because it's nice to show that the brainy girl can also be pretty . . . because when most people think of brainy girls, they think of a nerd and someone who's not very social."

COSTAR QUICKIES •
Vanessa's instant response to her castmates:

Zac: "Gorgeous!"
Lucas: "Character!"
Corbin: "Hair!"
Ashley: "Fun!"
Monique: "When I first met Monique, she had Corbin's hair!"
Chris: "I love Chris!"

Sister-2-Sister:

Vanessa's sister, Stella, is actually in *HSM* — "In the very beginning there are two little girls right behind me, and the one in the white dress is my sister. She's my mini-me. We listen to the same music, we dress the same — sometimes she's even way more fashionable than me and I end up saying, 'I have to change now, because you look too good.' She's just so much fun."

ON HEALTHY EATING . . .

"I don't go long without eating. I never starve myself: I grab a healthy snack."

ON BEING A BIG SISTER . . .

"I just think it's so great to be friends with a sibling because they are going to be there for you no matter what."

ON TEEN CHALLENGES:

"When I was thirteen, I did a movie called *Thirteen*, which was actually a controversial film. It was basically about wild teenagers who make the wrong decisions and take the wrong path. When kids are young, they want to experience things, but they don't see what the downside to it is. . . . I think that people really need to be educated about things like drugs and alcohol and what they can do to you in the long term. You just shouldn't do it; it's not something that's beneficial to you in the first place. Go out and shop if that makes you feel better, rather than doing something stupid or that you are pressured into doing."

VANESSA UP CLOSE

- Vanessa's favorite guilty pleasure is chocolate! — "You give me any kind of chocolate, I will eat it. I've always loved it ever since I was little. I even have it by my bed-side."
- Vanessa and Ashley love singing the songs from *Rent*.
- Vanessa loves Frankie B jeans.
- Vanessa's first big purchase was "a limited edition Dior purse when I was in London."
- Vanessa's dream car is a Porsche Carerra GT.
- Vanessa would love to go skydiving . . . just like Zac!
- Vanessa's favorite fast food joint is In-N-Out.
  - Vanessa loves to shop!
- Vanessa released her debut solo CD, V, on September 26, 2006.

- Vanessa made her big-screen acting debut in the film *Thirteen*, but she had appeared on TV's *Still Standing* before that.
- Vanessa would love to learn how to whistle!
- Vanessa's little sister, Stella, appeared in the 2006 movie *The Memory Thief*.
- If you check under Vanessa's bed, you will probably find her journal.
- While on the *HSM* promo visit to Australia, Vanessa went to a zoo, where she petted a kangaroo. The 'roo stood up and put up his paws and wanted to box Vanessa!

TO BEE OR NOT TO BEE!

"I don't like bees very much. I was at a photo shoot recently when all of a sudden I feel something hit me and I'm like, 'What in the world?' And I look down on my shirt and there's a bee! I started screaming!"

FRIENDS TO THE END!

"My best friend is actually Ashley Tisdale! . . . I originally met her on a commercial we did for Sears, where we were actually dancing as well. The first time we saw each other after we knew we had gotten *High School Musical* was in the recording studio. We just ran to each other, screamed, and jumped up and down like a pair of little girls. We were so excited!"

ASHLEY ON VANESSA

"She's the sweetest person. She'll be shopping, and if she sees something that looks like me, like Tinkerbell gifts [Ashley loves the Peter Pan character], she'll get it for me."

FAN-TASTIC!

When Vanessa and the gang attended a WNBA basketball game in Los Angeles, 150 fans surrounded them. "We were the Beatles — it was insane," says an amazed Vanessa.

ASHLEY TISDALE

ALL ABOUT ASHLEY

IF ASHLEY IS YOUR FAVE ... GET TO KNOW HER FABULOUS FAX!

FAVE-TASTICS

Sport: Basketball
TV show: *Laguna Beach*
Movie: *My Best Friend's Wedding*
Actresses: Brittany Murphy, Julia Roberts
Singer: Billy Joel
Car: Range Rover
Drink: Vanilla Blend from Coffee Bean
Fast food restaurant: McDonald's
Sandwich: Peanut butter & jelly
Fashion designer: Bebe
Holiday: Christmas
Family tradition: To watch *Miracle on 34th Street* with her family on Thanksgiving
Mom's recipe: Caesar salad
Room service order: Chocolate milkshakes

ASHLEY IN THE SPOTLIGHT

Full name: Ashley Michelle Tisdale
Nickname: Pookie or Pookernuts (her family gave her them)
B-Day: July 2, 1985
Birthplace: Neptune, New Jersey
Righty or Lefty: Ashley is left-handed
Parents: Lisa and Mike
Sibling: Older sister Jennifer Kelly Tisdale
Pets: Maltipoo named Blondie

ON THE MOVIE MESSAGE:

"The whole movie is about being yourself and not being in a clique. You don't have to be just one thing. Kids get stuck in a clique and can't get out of it. You feel people won't support you in anything else. I think it's important to find yourself in school and be happy about it, and if people don't support you, they're not your real friends."

ASHLEY'S POV:

On Sharpay: "Sharpay is the queen bee. That's how nuts she is — she's named after a dog! But all of a sudden things are changing and people are coming out of the cliques, so she's threatened."

On teen queens vs. brainiacs:

"Hollywood makes brainiac girls sort of plain but, in High School Musical, they're gorgeous. I'm glad girls get to see that it's not one or the other. They get to see that they can be pretty and smart."

ON GETTING THROUGH HIGH SCHOOL...
"Stay true to **yourself**. Don't follow the crowd."

ON FINDING OUT WHO YOU ARE...
"I feel like people expect a lot of girls, like you're **supposed** to know who you are and what you want out of life **right now**. Some girls know. I did. But lots of [girls] **don't** know. You have to try a lot of things and not worry about what people are **thinking**."

ON ACHIEVING GOALS...
"My parents told me to **follow my dreams** and to never give up no matter what happens or if things get hard. It is hard work, so just **keep focused** and never give up."

20

ASHLEY ABCS

- Ashley launched **Pink Twinkle** cosmetic line for Club Libby Lu. The Pink Twinkle tag line is "Sparkle, You're a Star."
- Ashley actually is a naturally **curly brunette**.
- Ashley would rather "have a sleepover or go bowling with girl friends" than go clubbing with Hollywood **hotties**!
- Ashley's **best friend** is her older sister, actress Jennifer Tisdale.
- Ashley worked at Abercrombie & Fitch, Hollister, Windsor, and Wet Seal in local malls when she took a short break between high school and more acting projects.

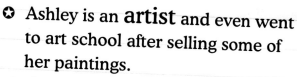

- Ashley is an **artist** and even went to art school after selling some of her paintings.
- Ashley released her **debut CD** for Warner Bros. Records in 2007.

CELEBRITY CRUSH

"I think Jake Gyllenhaal is so cute. If I ever talked to him, I'd end up giggling!"

ASHLEY MAKES HISTORY

Ashley has made a major music industry name for herself — she is the first female singer to have two singles debut at the same time on the *Billboard* Hot 100 — "Bop to the Top" and "What I've Been Looking For" from the *High School Musical* soundtrack.

CORBIN BLEU

CRUSH ON CORBIN!

IF CORBIN **MOVES AND GROOVES** YOU ... HERE'S AN UP CLOSE AND **PERSONAL** LOOK!

FAVE-TASTICS

Sports: Basketball
Movies: *Chicago, Bad Boys II*
Actor: Johnny Depp
Car: Porsche Spider
Food: French fries
Fast food restaurant: In-N-Out
Candy: Twix
Sandwich: Sausage and peppers
Pizza topping: Pepperoni
Colors: Gold and black — especially if it is a leopard print. "Most of the stuff in my room is in leopard print," admits Corbin.
Hi-tech toy: His cell phone — a Treo 650 from Verizon
School subject: Science — "I love doing experiments in the lab."
Book: *The Great Gatsby* by F. Scott Fitzgerald
Author: J. K. Rowling
Article of clothing: His beat-up leather jacket

CORBIN COUNTDOWN

Full name: Corbin Bleu Reivers
Stage name: Corbin Bleu
Nickname: Bleuman
B-Day: February 21, 1989
Birthplace: Brooklyn, New York
Righty or Lefty: Corbin is right-handed
Parents: David and Martha
Siblings: Younger sisters Hunter, Phoenix, Jag

22

On Chad:

"Chad is very into basketball. I'm similar to Chad in the way that he has a strong passion for what he does. But I'm kinda sports-challenged. Give me a ball and I don't know what to do with the thing! But I worked really hard and by the end I was very comfortable with the ball."

On the movie's mega success:

"It's become a huge phenomenon and it's something we're very excited to be a part of. It's just one of those things that we weren't expecting. Now that we're here, we're amazed."

SUDS SAGA

"It makes me cry when I run out of shampoo!"

On His Audition:

"I actually originally auditioned for Lucas's role, Ryan. As it turned out, I couldn't shake my hips as well as Lucas could. It turned out that they felt I was better for the role of Chad. I ended up going in for that role and they loved me."

CORBIN'S POV:

On Chad and Troy's friendship: "It's not one of those things where they just met in high school. They are friends from kindergarten and elementary school. They grew up together . . . Chad will totally put Troy in a headlock and give him a noogie. I wanted him to be as relaxed as possible around Troy, because Troy is family to him."

CORBIN UP CLOSE

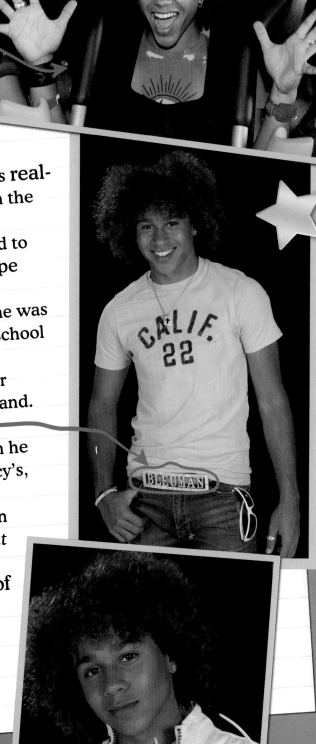

- Corbin admits he was a "wild thing!" when he was a little kid.
- Describing himself today, Corbin says: "I am secure with who I am. I march to the **beat of my own drum**."
- Corbin's second Disney Channel movie was *Jump In*, in which he costarred with Keke (*Akeelah and the Bee*) Palmer. His real-life dad, David Reivers, played his dad in the film!
- For his role as "Izzy" in *Jump In*, Corbin had to train in both boxing and double-dutch rope jumping.
- Corbin admits he was embarrassed when he was voted **"teacher's pet"** in his high school year book.
- The first trip out of the country for Corbin was to Jamaica, his father's homeland.
- Corbin collects **belt buckles.**
- Corbin began his career as a toddler when he appeared in commercials and ads for Macy's, GAP, Target and Toys "R" Us.
- Corbin's **first lead role** in a movie was in *Catch That Kid* (2004) and on TV in *Flight 29 Down* (2005).
- While attending **Los Angeles School of Arts**, Corbin starred in productions of *Footloose* as "Ren" and *Grease* as "Sonny."
- Corbin's dad is an actor — David Reivers — who appeared in the 2006 movie *Poseidon*.

CORBIN'S TEEN SURVIVAL GUIDE

ON MAKING A MISTAKE . . .
"Everyone feels embarrassed, but when you laugh it off, it's fine."

ON AVOIDING FIGHTS . . .
"Never throw the first punch and try not to throw the second!"

ON LEARNING SOMETHING NEW . . . "Listen. Always listen. Everyone and everything always has something to offer. Listen to it. Absorb it. Apply it."

ALL IN THE NAME

Bleu is Corbin's real middle name and Corbin's parents followed the "color" theme for his younger sisters — Hunter Grey, Phoenix Sage, and Jag Sienna. "With the two little ones, Phoenix and Jag, we actually took out crayon boxes and looked at the different colors," recalls Corbin.

NEAT FREAK
"Everything is exactly in place [in my room]. The books and CDs aren't just put away, they're in alphabetical order and everything is perfectly straightened."

SURF'S UP
"I'm a beach person. I love the water! I swear I'm a fish!"

LUCAS GRABEEL

THE LUCK OF LUCAS

IF YOU ARE **IN LOVE** WITH LUCAS . . . COMMIT THIS INFO TO **MEMORY!**

TICKET ADMIT ONE

LUCAS'S LIST

Full name: Lucas Stephen Grabeel
B-Day: November 23, 1984
Birthplace: Springfield, Missouri
Parents: Stephen and Jean
Sibling: Older sister Autumn
Schools: Logan-Rogersville Elementary and Middle School, Kickapoo High School, and Missouri Fine Arts Academy
Pet: Lilly, a Maltese poodle — she actually is his sister's dog

27

WHEN I WAS IN SCHOOL...

"Everyone perceived me as being **different** from who I was. I said, 'You know what, it's gonna be okay, because I'm gonna trudge through these years and really find what **I want to do.** I won't allow anything to hold me back and pretty much **go for** one hundred and ten percent.'"

IF YOU WANT TO BECOME AN ACTOR...

"Whatever **age** you are, the most important thing is to get involved and **get experience.** The teachers can teach you, but try to **audition** for a play or a performing troupe. A lot of people think that actors don't have to be **smart**—but I say read a lot because knowledge is **power.** Be as well-versed in as much as you can, and you will be better in **any career** that you choose."

MY ADVICE FOR TEENS...

"Really believe in **yourself** and believe in your product whatever **your product** is, whatever makes you **happy** and believe that whatever you think about is **going to happen.** Thinking and believing are two different things, so believe it, and it will come **true.**"

28

ON THE AUDITION:

"It was a lot like a theatrical audition . . . So it was a weird throwback [for me]. I got right into it and had a lot of fun. It was ambiguous at the beginning regarding what *HSM* was going to be, because we had a short script and did not hear any of the music. I thought it was just another audition and just went in there and did my thing. A month later, I found out I was cast."

FAN REACTION:

"Everywhere I go now, someone says something. It's at the movie theater, at the bank, pretty much any public place that kids could be. [Once when I was in Malibu] a girl came up to me, and stood in front of me with her mouth wide open. She couldn't say anything. These kids are really excited about [*High School Musical*]. It's a big deal for them."

On Ryan:

"I hope that I am nothing like my character. He is very much into looking his best, always being in fashion and always thinking about his personal appearance and his sister's personal appearance and well-being."

LUCAS TIDBITS

- When Lucas first moved to Los Angeles to become an **actor**, he supported himself working at **Blockbuster**.
- Lucas is not a big **pop music** fan — he likes different kinds of music, even **country-western**.
- Lucas appeared in the **TV movies** *In the Blink of an Eye, Halloweentown High, Halloweentown: Witch U,* and *High School Musical.*
- If Lucas was offered a biopic, he would like to play Nirvana's **Kurt Cobain** — "because I want [to play] someone who has **mysteries**."
- Lucas lives in an apartment in Sherman Oaks, CA, with his **sister Autumn** and her boyfriend.
- Lucas plays the **guitar** and drums.
- Lucas met his manager, **Robert C. Thompson**, at a mall — they were both in line waiting to buy a **smoothie**.
- Lucas's best friends are his **hometown buddies** Michael Brown and Marc Blackwell — they run Lucas's **website**.
- Lucas and his mom like to watch **classic films** like *Singin' in the Rain* and *White Christmas.*

ADMIT ONE

Lucas's Hometown:
Springfield, Missouri. Springfield is the third largest city in Missouri. Springfield was founded in 1829. Springfield is known as "the Birthplace of Route 66."

Lucas did a music video for Disney's DVD, *The Fox and the Hound.*

THE REAL LUCAS
"I am a simple, plain person. You know, I'm chilled and laid back and not so out there and crazy."

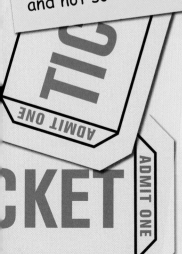

MOVIE BUFF
"When I worked at Blockbuster I had a sweet hookup — they gave me free rentals occasionally!"

MONIQUE COLEMAN

MONIQUE MANIA

IF MONIQUE IS THE **ACTRESS/DANCER/SINGER** OF YOUR **DREAMS** ... GET TO KNOW HER **PERSONAL STYLE**

MONIQUE TO THE MAX
Full name: Monique Coleman
B–Day: November 13, 1980
Birthplace: Orangeburg, South Carolina
Parent: Mother, Roz Coleman
College: De Paul University in Chicago — graduated in 2002

TICKET
ADMIT ONE

MONIQUE'S POV:

ON TAYLOR: "Taylor is the president of the chemistry club and the head of the scholastic decathlon, as well as best friends with Gabriella. And my character is a little bit brighter in the math and science department than I am . . . okay, a lot!"

ON MONIQUE'S CASTMATES: "We are really like family, and I really get along with everyone. We see a lot of one another. One of the things I am proud of is that we have avoided the tendency to have cliques among us."

ON MONIQUE'S AUDITION . . . "I'm the only character that doesn't sing in the movie. I originally auditioned for the role of Gabriella, and I do have a bit of stage fright that I overcame by doing this movie. . . . At that first *a capella* audition, I ended up in the corner with my back to the casting directors, singing to myself in the corner because I was so afraid. When I was done, I had this feeling that I wouldn't reduce myself to this, so I turned around and said, 'I am such a better actress than this.' . . . A month later I was called back for Taylor."

ON THE MOVIE'S BEST DANCER . . . "Corbin Bleu. He danced with Debbie Allen when he was a kid."

ON SKIN CARE PRODUCTS . . .

"I don't really use **expensive** products or anything. I love the **oil-free Clean & Clear** deep cleanser and I use **Bobbi Brown** moisturizer. And I love Dermalogica exfoliant....I love Bobbi Brown foundation and concealer and their liners. But for **eye color**, **MAC is it.**"

ON SETTING FUTURE GOALS . . . "Do your **own thing;** always follow your dreams and **don't feel limited** by what someone prescribes to you as to what you **should do.** Expand your horizons, try new things, be **adventurous.**"

ON BEING A ROLE MODEL . . .

"It's definitely a **responsibility** and one that [the entire cast] stepped up to the plate. Especially for me and my character — **the smart girl....** I think it is important for girls to see movies where it is not all just **about 'the boy'** or it's simply about **'the relationship'** or 'Am I pretty enough?' or 'Am I **cute enough?'** Here [in the movie] is something that has to do with 'Am I talented enough?' or 'Am I smart enough?' **I love that.** It is a big responsibility but it's **exciting.**"

ON FITTING IN . . . "Have the confidence not to be like **everybody else,** to be alone, to stand up for **yourself** and to know that ultimately hard work does **pay off** in the end."

TICKET
ADMIT ONE

MONIQUE UNDER THE MAGNIFYING GLASS

- ✪ Monique's **all-time** favorite movie musical is *Fame* — "*Fame* is the movie that made me want to be an actress. When I saw *Fame*, I said, 'I do not just want to be a **spectator**, but to be a **part of it.**'"
- ✪ Monique's favorite **theatrical musical** is *Big River*.
- ✪ Monique would **love** to play Left Eye in a biopic on the group TLC.
- ✪ Monique has a recurring role as Mary Margaret on *The Suite Life of Zack & Cody*.
- ✪ Monique loves to go **hiking and camping.**
- ✪ Monique received a 2006 **Camie Award** for her role as **Leesha** in the Hallmark movie, *The Reading Room.*
- ✪ Monique loves **all kinds** of music — Donny Hathaway, Al Green, Bill Withers, OutKast, Black Eyed Peas, Beyoncé.

HEALTHY MONIQUE
"If I was told I could never be an actress again, I would want to be in alternative medicine."

DANCING WITH MONIQUE
Monique was one of the celebrity competitors on the third season of ABC's *Dancing With the Stars*.

MONIQUE'S HOMETOWN:
Orangeburg, South Carolina. Orangeburg was founded in 1704. Orangeburg is known as "Garden City." Orangeburg has an annual "Festival of Flowers."

SMART IS HOT
"Above all, believe in yourself. Believe in anything you are capable of doing. Study hard. Don't just rely on natural talent."

TICKET

ADMIT ONE

CHRIS WARREN, JR.

COOKIE CUTEY

IF CHRIS IS YOUR **SWEETIE** ... EAT UP THESE SNACKS!

CHRIS TOP-TO-TOE

Full name: Christopher King Oneal Warren, Jr.

Nickname: L.C. — it stands for "little Chris" so people won't confuse him with his dad, Christopher Warren, Sr.

B-Day: January 15, 1990

Birthplace: Indianapolis, Indiana

Parents: Christopher Warren, Sr. and Brook Kerr

Righty or Lefty: Chris is right-handed

Pet: A Pomeranian dog

College plans: Wants to go to UCLA to study business

ON THE SEQUEL... "I am still **trying to** get with Sharpay and still **trying** to do the baking thing."

ON HIS FAVORITE SCENE... "After the credits with Ashley and me — when she says she **likes my cookies** and then tackles me and I make some *crème brûlée*. That scene was written, but we didn't think we were going to do it. It **barely** made the cut at the very end. It was Ashley's last scene before she went back to California. We only did it **two or three** times. It was close to the end of the day and we had to get **out of** there."

FAVE-TASTICS

Sports: Football, basketball, baseball
Sports team: Indianapolis Colts
TV show: *Entourage*
Actors/Actress: His dad, Christopher Warren; his mom, Brook Kerr; Denzel Washington, Derek Luke
Food: Pizza
Fast food restaurant: Wendy's
Drink: Cherry Coke
Candy: Twix
Sandwich: Chicken club
Chewing gum: Big Red
Color: Red

CHRIS'S CHECK LIST

- ✪ Chris played "Jimmy Ramirez" on the soap opera *The Bold and the Beautiful.*
- ✪ Chris plays running back and linebacker on his **high school football** team.
- ✪ Chris would **love** to play Walter "Sweetness" Payton in a biopic. The late Walter Payton was a **NFL super-star** who played for the Chicago Bears.
- ✪ Chris played the "**young Simba**" in *The Lion King* on Broadway and in the touring company.
- ✪ Chris can do **different accents** easily — when he was only 4 years old, he imitated his dad, who was practicing a dialogue with a Scottish accent. "It was **perfect**," says Chris's dad.

THE GIRL THING

"I like a girl to have a good personality and be outgoing, because I am hyper and have a good personality. They definitely have to have a sense of humor."

ANDREW SEELEY

Nickname: Drew

Claim to fame: Was credited with singing the Zac (Troy Bolton) Efron songs in *High School Musical.* Andrew sang Troy/Zac's solos. It was reported that Zac only sang the beginning and the end of the songs because he could not hit the higher notes. Insiders described it as "blending" the two singers' voices.

B-Day: April 30, 1982

Birthplace: Ottawa, Canada

Hometown: Toronto, Canada

Fave sports: Hockey, skiing

Acting career: Drew has been acting/singing since he was ten years old. At age eleven he did a revival of *Showboat* in Toronto. He also appeared on Broadway and made guest appearances on *One Tree Hill, Dawson's Creek,* and *The Guiding Light.*

Big break: *High School Musical*

Next step: Sings "Dance With Me" in *Cheetah Girls 2*

Films: *Christopher Brennan Saves the World, Campus Confidential, Locusts!*

Fave musical artists: Stevie Wonder, Maroon 5, Donny Hathaway

His style of music: "Something based in soul."

Instrument: Guitar

"I would like to have a career similar to Prince and Lauryn Hill. . . . I understand branding, and I understand you want to get out to as many people. But at the same time, artists today, and movie stars too, people in the spotlight, there's no mystique around them, because they're just everywhere you look. People like Lauryn Hill and Prince — they don't give interviews very often, you still feel like you don't know everything about them. I think that's kind of exciting. I want to just make the best album that I can possibly make, make movies that are really meaningful to me. . . . I don't want to work just to work."

We're not done yet — here are OODLES more fun stats on *High School Musical*!

HSM NUMBERS & AWARDS

- ✪ On January 20, 2006, when *High School Musical* first debuted on the Disney Channel, **7.7 million viewers** tuned in — more than **any other** original cable TV movie!

- ✪ **Future airings** of *HSM* increased the audience to over 40 million tune-ins!

- ✪ When the Disney Channel aired the sing-along version of *HSM*, it was the **number one** show for kids 6-11!
- ✪ When the *High School Musical* soundtrack was released on January 10, 2006, it debuted at #143 on the *Billboard* 200 chart. It hit the **number one spot** twice in March 2006.
- ✪ The *HSM* soundtrack has been **certified multi-platinum.**
- ✪ The *HSM* soundtrack hit the **top-spot** on the iTunes Best Selling Albums.
- ✪ The *HSM* soundtrack also hit the **number one spot** on Amazon.com's top sellers for music.

ADMIT ONE

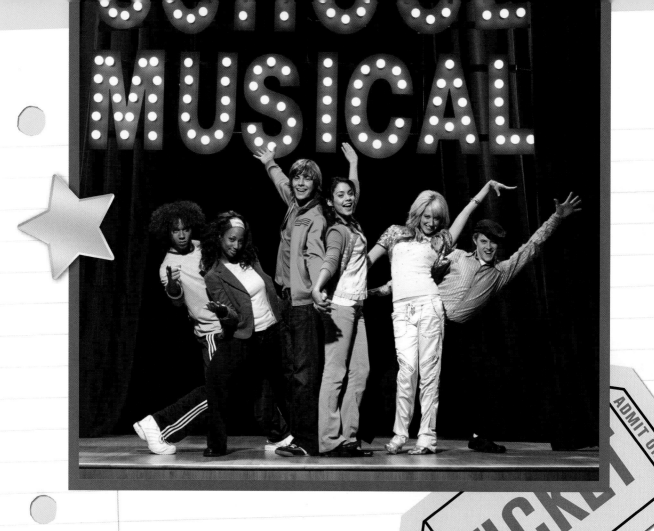

- The *HSM* soundtrack had **five singles** in the Top 40 on *Billboard*'s Hot 100 list.
- The *HSM* soundtrack is the first album from a TV show that went to the **Number One** spot on *Billboard*'s charts since *Miami Vice*.
- The *High School Musical* DVD came out on May 23, 2006 — in the first 5 weeks on sale, it sold **2.1 million** copies.
- *High School Musical* is a worldwide **phenomenon** — over 100 countries have aired the TV movie.
- The debut of *HSM* on UK TV on September 25, 2006, was a **smash hit** — over **1 million** viewers tuned in!
- The book *High School Musical — the Novel*, debuted on the *New York Times* bestsellers's list and **in two weeks** reached the number one spot.